FROM THE BOX MARKED
SOME ARE MISSING

FROM THE BOX MARKED
SOME ARE MISSING

Charles W. Pratt

The Hobblebush Granite State Poetry Series, Volume I

HOBBLEBUSH BOOKS

Brookline, New Hampshire

Composed in Adobe Arno Pro
at Hobblebush Books

Printed in the United States of America

Cover photograph by Sidney Hall Jr.

ISBN: 978-0-9801672-8-3

Library of Congress Control Number: 2010928484

The Hobblebush Granite State Poetry Series, Volume I
Editors: Sidney Hall Jr. and Rodger Martin

HOBBLEBUSH BOOKS
17-A Old Milford Road
Brookline, New Hampshire 03033

www.hobblebush.com

CONTENTS

◇
◇ From *In the Orchard* (1986) ◇
◇

IN THE WOODS

What's he doing, you'd wonder, here in the very
Middle of the woods, shouldering logs from a stack
Someone cut and left so long ago
How could it promise any significant heat
Across two hundred branch-littered, bouldery
Yards to drop them onto a raggeder heap?
Forth and back, forth again and back
Over pine needles and crunchy patches of snow,
Log's weight pressing his feet into every
Irregularity of terrain, nose to the sweet
Heavy fungus smell of sodden bark, he keeps
Going. And when a log slips from his shoulder
At last, like guilt or a cherished injury,
For a moment he's almost light enough to fly.

LEARNING TO PRUNE

I bless thee, Lord, because I grow
Among the trees, which in a row
To thee both fruit and order owe.
— GEORGE HERBERT, "PARADISE"

Jock perches in the top
of the apple like a wild
turkey (I've seen them here),
the sound of his saw
nastying a little the nice
March day: south slope, false spring.
I, on the ground,
circle my tree slowly,
reaching my long pole-clippers up
to the suckers and branches I want
out. My neck aches as I
jerk the handle and a branch
drops. It snags, I flip it clear.
I had it in mind this morning
I'd get a poem out of pruning,
about discipline, I thought, and form,
like Herbert's "Paradise"—
but Jock has taught me already
it's not a question of that so much
as of opening up the center
to sun and air, taking out what
grows too upright or crosses,
and keeping the top in reach.
He's down from the tree now, his clippers
snick quickly, he talks
to himself as he works.

Each time I finish a tree,
maybe one to three of his,
he comes over to check,
snips a little here and there,
and tells me I'm doing fine,
though I cut more than he would, probably,
on a Cortland, that is;
you can let a Cortland grow thicker; with Cortlands
people don't mind a little green on the apple,
but they like their Macs red.
Towards 5:00—I'm tired, but
ready to go on as long as he can—
he says it's time to quit.
We go in and drink hot tea
with honey, talk a bit,
and then he's off, clipper pole
poking from the Volkswagen's open window.
A few more days like this with him,
he says, and I'll have the swing of it,
I'll be on my own.

STONES

Mowing the old field, he thinks mostly
Of stones, boulders really, knucklebones
Of buried giants, porpoises
Somersaulting through the surf of earth,
Playful as porpoises the way they break
His blades if he's careless. But that's *his*
Fancy, he knows; it's not they who play
With him but he with them, at least
Those he can see, shaving them close
And fast as he dares. Other times only
Memory or a tuft of higher grass
Reminds him where they are in time to
Swerve where granite bulges. So
Hawk's shadow crossing his shoulder, clouds'
Metamorphoses he ignores; stones
Keep his eyes low to study
The way the land lies, the grass grows.
They wait, they do nothing, they give
Only themselves, their one assertion:
Stone. And he is grateful for them,
Presences he can almost count on.

ANSWERING THE QUESTIONS

He looks up from his shingling and squints over
The valley where the hidden river runs.
"I wouldn't mind retiring here myself."
"Neither would I,"

I answer drily, but wonder whether I have
In giving up my paycheck to live off
Land and wife in a state of antisocial
Insecurity.

150 apple trees, three garden plots,
Dirt-crammed fingernails and a stiff back
Are my evidence that this is no pulling out
But a digging in,

No retreat but a strategic withdrawal
From territory too long occupied,
No longer friendly, not worth holding on to,
To advance on a new front.

The reporter shuts his notebook. Unconvinced?
Print this, I tell him, this is the one thing that matters:
Whatever the pressures, I have retracted nothing,
And will not retract.

He's gone back to hammering on the roof,
I go back to digging in the garden,
And the river goes on running through the valley,
Unobserved.

Spray or Pray

With apples, it's either
Spray or pray, I'm told, and feeling
Ill-at-ease with both, but being,
I guess, inevitably 20th century,
Choose to spray. 5:00 AM,
Before the wind rises to spread
Poison where it isn't wanted,
Dressed like an astronaut or lunatic
Religious in hooded
Waterproof, respirator, goggles,
I drive my tractor from tree to tree,
Dragging the tank of noxious stuff
I've reluctantly weighed and mixed.
I dismount, point the spraygun upwards,
And squeeze the trigger: a vague
Haze drifts over tree,
Grass, sprayer, tractor, me,
Fogs my goggles till I stumble
As though through some foreign element.
Hating the poison, hating the noisy
Sprayer engine which quits from time to time
Just to remind me who's in control,
Hating the sun which dazzles
And steams me in my waterproof,
Hating the wind, hating even
The apple trees and especially
My own incompetent self,
I half do what they say I must do,
And hope without faith that it will make

Some difference. (In fact,
The apples are scabby anyway,
But I've killed the worst pests,
Plum curculios and maggots.)
In what, then, *do* I have faith,
The way, at night, going from barn to house,
The body knows its way without misstep:
Assumes the invisible orchard?

GREED AND GRACE IN THE ORCHARD

The druid priestess, capitalist to the core,
Who sold the orchard to us didn't know,
Or didn't choose to tell,
That down in the hollow by the well
Among the chokecherry and juniper
Wild blueberries grow.

Whether she thought bushes inferior
Gods, or the berries too small and few
For profit, she consigned
Us gratis the pleasures of both find
And fruit. And when the tractor that she swore
Was good as new

Wheel-deep in daisies is dreaming like Ferdinand,
Some inner organ broken beyond my skill,
While maggot flies lay
Eggs in the apples I can't spray,
Or weeds in the garden have gotten the upper hand,
I go downhill

To the nets I've spread—just outcast from the commune
Of the wild—to keep the catbirds in their place,
And crouched in the stagnant air
Pick until every bush is bare
And berries fill my bowl with unearned income,
Nature's grace.

Mosquitoes seethe in the bottom. As I sweat and slap,
I imagine blueberry midnight. The moon is full,
And the priestess, naked, dances
Before her trees, which stretch out branches
Trembling with the bumper crop of apples
Fattening to fall.

THE QUIET OF THE COUNTRY

The baseboard cricket's at it again,
Playing and playing his one refrain,
As constant as a shrewish wife
Who's condemned herself to you for life,
At it, at it, at it again,
At it again and again until
You, too, are single-minded: kill
The baseboard cricket at it again,
At it, at it, at it again.

≈

All summer, one by one,
The apples drop. We shudder
At the impact in the bone

As if, far off, big guns
Echoed from war long over
Or war still to begin.

≈

Seen from this hilltop, stars
At eye level quiver in the night.
Looking through branches, you'd guess airplanes,
But watch a while and they still keep their place.

Right the first time, of course. They race
Burning through space, roaring like the dragstrip
Four miles away, where under crackling lights
Pickupsful chug beer and cheer the cars.

ON THE BEAUTY OF THE UNIVERSAL ORDER

Odd
to think that God
designed
the apple tree
so perfectly
to catch on crooked branch, in acute crotch
the narrow pointed ladder Adam would invent
to ease his labors when as punishment
for apple-snatching, he was sent
forth wandering from the garden. Odd that I,
without design,
at least of mine,
now at the end of almost fifty years should find
myself here high
on springy rungs, the ladder like an arrow pointing me
towards dangling planets. I grasp a branch and lean
over the void to grip
the perfect apple at the branch's tip.

Brown
below my feet, turned earth tells where
this morning I clawed down
ladderless to find
and fumble up to air,
knobby and bare
as baby skulls, huge as pre-Edenic continents,
my Kennebecs:
earth-apples. One,
under my hand,
stirred, shook off a clod,
became bloat toad.
Also child of God.

HARVEST

The trees, I'm told, have stood here fifty years—
Bearers still. The motherly Cortlands, fat
As their dusky apples, cookers, firm in pies.
The Macs more upright, sparer, the apples—
This year, at least—scarcer, smaller, brighter,
Flecked with little lights. And the Wageners,
Bristling with apples from a thousand spurs,
The fruit a modest russet, turning as it ripens
To scarlet, apples from a Book of Hours.

≈

Sweetness seethes from the press, foams
In the bucket; I turn with the handle
Under the mild October sun
That brings back summer, softened. Sun-yellow
Hornets, now, mellowed from when,
In August, the mower brought their stinging
Hubbub up from underground,
Nuzzle my sticky fingers, gentle as cows,
Swoon to that foaming sweetness where they drown.

≈

Midnight, midwinter. Under the full moon
The trees, like twisting smoke, like rocks
Whorled by tides of air,
Stand stock-still in their shadows
On the new snow, precise and mysterious
As spiders on a linen tablecloth.
Arrested, I look out, investing
Them with the patient merit
And deliberate innocence I would learn of them.

INTERLUDE

The sun slips lower. Yesterday it snowed—
A frozen inch or two: enough. For now
Forget the maul and wedge, the unsplit wood,
All that you *should* for winter, grab the cracked sled
(Plastic) from the barn, run, leap . . . slide,
Belly flattened to the hard hill's hide—
Mad bronco bucking till the cowboy's spilled,
Mad lover answering hips with surging hips—
While orderly ranks of apples stand appalled,
Black-robed widows, blurring with your speed,
And westward the sunset, row on row, applauds
In frenzied violets, crimsons. Now the sled slows,
Stops. Bring in the wood. Tonight, deep cold.

Exercise of the Imagination

To go to sleep, he said, when you have insomnia,
Imagine a field of perfect white; and whenever
Anything appears in the field, erase it. And then erase the eraser.
I try to imagine it that way: the orchard as it is at this moment,
The particular light of this November afternoon, the way that
       the light
Now, at this instant, turns the small crinkled apple leaves orange,
       not bright
Orange, but warm, an orange that somehow insists
In the heart on the importance of this instant, of each particular
       instant,
And the clouds piling up to the east there, over the woods, and
       the slope of the falling
Of that leaf in the wind against the slope of the hill
Erased
As by deep December snow—so deep as to ungrass the slope,
       untree the woods, unbird the sky, unsky the universe, white,
       white, and then that white
Erased,
All consciousness of white erased by white . . .

And when you are asleep, black, black—not the sleep of dreams
But the sleep between dreams, the single snap of the fingers
That takes you through who knows what void, what space of
       time to morning . . .

And if there is no morning?

       The long disgrace
Of history erased . . .

       And all that we see,
All that our beautiful seeing makes beautiful.

THE GIFT

after a stained-glass window by Gabriel Loire

In Gabriel's window, Eve offers the apple again,
And could Adam refuse
Her on her knees raising the apple bright
As heart's blood, as hearth-fire?
The fish approves, the donkey, the ram, the dove,
A shimmer of blues
Overhead; and the snake is winding around them the golden
Coils of desire.
Fear not—it is Gabriel's voice in the throats of the flowers:
The flesh is sweet.
Be joyful, fear not, for you are filled with the light.
Take the apple, and eat.

WINTER SQUASH

In bare December, the spirit seeks out matter.
You turn from the window and go down to the cellar,
Past braids of onions hanging from the rafters,
Sacks of potatoes and carrots, boxes of apples,
To stroke the hard smooth skin of the winter squashes,
Tawny butternut and ribbed green acorn,
Row after row on shelves, like words in Webster's,
Waiting. You pick one up. Sun on your shoulder
Weighs as you stoop to plant, to weed, to water.
Cool and dark, you stand in the buried cellar
Forming your sentence, then climb back up to winter.

THE BLISS OF BEARS

for Cabot Lyford

A bear on a raspberry bender, Vermont friends say,
Lies on his back and squirms headfirst through the stalks
Like a bulldozer flattening trees for a porkbarrel highway,
Clawing the berries down into ravenous jaws.
He stains his fur coat blood-purple as he blunders backwards,
Nothing on earth but his gullet he gives a damn for—
Why should he worry? He'll be asleep all winter;
No freezer to fill, no neighbors to put up jam for.
He didn't set out this patch—didn't weed it or thin it,
Maybe manured it one day just passing by,
But gave it never a thought until he was in it,
Backstroking bearwise, gazing up at the sky,
Which dangles over his nose its ripe red riches
While earth underneath him curries his ticks and itches.

FIBONACCI SEQUENCE

Stars,

as

we see

them at least,

refuse to keep their

distances, prefer company,

declare themselves chairs, bears, dippers, sweet milky highways.

So the hermit is sustained, isn't he, in dark privacy by the invisible

strings by which he dangles from the high hand of his God?

So many bees stinging night's flesh!

The passion of all

singleness

to keep

in

touch.

RELATIVITY

for Lotte Jacobi

As we go down in the dark the slight
Icy slope to the car, the grip of your hands
On my shoulders tells me you're right

Behind me and upright. I don't understand
Relativity, but forty-some years ago
You photographed Albert Einstein, and

Today I saw his soft eyes, below
The fine accumulation of his hair,
Random, gentle, abstract hair, as though

His thought like pipesmoke issued on the air;
I saw his sailboat drifting, his violin
Waiting his hands. And always I felt you there,

About the age I am you must have been,
Holding your camera as if you took a friend
By the shoulders to show him something you'd seen.

If the universe is a slope all things descend,
If the speed of light is the only absolute,
What every atom dreams of as its end,

On this icy path, if I should slip, would we shoot
Like lasers into the dark, a double star?
Old hands on my shoulders, be my parachute,

Help me go slow. And so we reach the car,
Waiting to take us wherever we're headed tonight,
And laughing, say to each other, "Here we are!"

DRIVING TO CAPE COD

Summers, when he drove us to Cape Cod,
My father missed red lights, abruptly stopped
For green. His eyes kept wandering from the road:
He'd see a heron stoic in a bog,
A fold of field, a woods, pronounce them good;
Converse with my mother till his foot forgot
The pressure of progress and the old coupe slowed—

Thirty-five, thirty . . . We itched, but Father knew
We had all summer to spend beside the point,
Stopped at a slow green light. He's dead now,
And caught between cars on the Interstate, intent
On a strip of macadam laid down like the Law,
So much attention focussed on accident,
How can his children see the things he saw?

THIRTY-FIVE

Thirty-five: reaching the outer curve
And turning back, beginning to enclose.
Conserve, an instinct cautions me, conserve:
Water and weed your acre, watch what grows.
The wall around your garden is the price
That must be paid for any paradise.
Another instinct answers that to live
Demands a wall as sensitive as skin—
At sixty let me have a lover's nerve
To let the inside out, the outside in.

The Infestation

All summer long
big ants have crawled
from our bedroom wall
like dirty words.
We squashed them first
in Kleenex, squirming,
and flushed them down
the toilet; then
when we began
to sense them on
our skin at night,
their feather-feet
more gentle than
our gentlest touch,
we crushed them flat
with books, with shoes,
barefoot, between
index and thumb,
till knotted corpses
glutted the rug
like ace after crumpled
ace of clubs.
Now when we see
an ant appear
and strangely reel
across our floor,
we let him go
in peace to wear
his poison vest,
like the emperor's clothes,

back to the nest,
where the other ants
can lick him clean.
My love, I taste
you in the night,
we twist and turn
and fall asleep,
while death goes on
behind the wall,
at last discreet.

FOR SARAH

you are twelve   you are lovely
still as a stone
in a Japanese garden
never still
you laugh, you cry, you go out
with Amy, with Pam   you come in
you are here   you are there
you are neither here nor there
at night you sleep
I kiss your cheek on the pillow
it is imponderable
you are a grey bird on the beach, a yellow bird
in my maple, moving
behind moving leaves
I cannot fix you
in my glasses, and when I do
I do not recognize you

EVENING MEDITATION IN A CATHEDRAL TOWN

Transparent on transparency,
A lacewing on the windowpane.
Pale green traceries of vein
In the lancets of its wings sustain
A membrane too fine for the eye.
As tranquil on the mystery
Of glass as if taught by its wings
How to put faith in invisible things,
In slow sweeps back and forth it swings
Its frail antennae thoughtfully,
Like compasses that leave no mark:
Geometers imagining the arc.

In the cathedral treasury
I've gazed, unmoved, at the Virgin's shift,
Draped like dead insect wings—enough,
The histories repeat, to lift
That heap of masonry so high.
Others believed in it; now I
Where the great stained windows raise
Their winged parabolas of praise
Day after day can bring to graze,
Sheepish, my agnostic eye.
Such precious straining of the light
Surprises stone and souls of stone to flight.

Small concentration of the evening air,
Lacewing, I look through you and glass to where
Beyond the fields the late sun condescends
To denseness, and its true brightness bends
And bursts to beauty where the transparent ends.

From *Fables in Two Languages and Similar Diversions* (1994)

L'Oiseau, la Souris, et le Chat

Un petit oiseau chantait
Sous le soleil de mai—
«Qu'il fait beau, qu'il fait beau, fait beau!»
Une souris lui chuchota,
«Ne sais-tu pas que le chat
Cherche par-ci, par-là,
Un morceau tendre comme toi?
Les petits doivent se taire. C'est la loi!»
L'oiseau chanta encore plus haut—
«Qu'il fait beau, qu'il fait beau, fait beau!»
Un jour vint le chat et mangea
Notre ami l'oiseau. Voilà,
Plus de chansons dans les champs,
On n'entend que le clac-clac des dents.
Et puis le chat prit la souris
Malgré les bons conseils soumis;
Il la mangea, c'est bien dommage,
Bien qu'elle fût silencieuse et sage.
La leçon qu'on apprend—qu'est-ce que c'est?
Qui ne chante jamais, ne chantera jamais.

The Bird, the Mouse, and the Cat

A little bird warbled away,
 Gay in the sunlight of May—
"What a day, what a day, day, day!"
"Psst!" hissed a mouse. "Keep it low!
 Mister Pussy's out prowling, you know.
 He's quite keen of hearing, and oh!
 How morsels like you make him drool.
 The small must keep still. That's the rule."
The bird sang still louder, "Hooray!
 What a day, what a day, day, day!"
One morning, along came the cat
And caught our friend bird. That was that.
A muffled chomp-chomp, and done!
 No more songs in the sun.
And next the cat ate—it's not nice—
Despite all its careful advice,
The mouse—popped it into the hopper,
Though so perfectly silent and proper.
The lesson you'll learn, if you're clever?
 If you don't ever sing, you won't ever.

LE CHAT

Viens, mon beau chat, sur mon coeur amoureux;
      Retiens les griffes de ta patte,
Et laisse-moi plonger dans tes beaux yeux
      Mêlés de métal et d'agate.

Lorsque mes doigts caressent à loisir
      Ta tête et ton dos élastique
Et que ma main s'enivre du plaisir
      De palper ton corps électrique,

Je vois ma femme en esprit; son regard,
      Comme le tien, aimable bête,
Profond et froid, coupe et fend comme un dard,

      Et des pieds jusques à la tête,
Un air subtil, un dangereux parfum,
      Nagent autour de son corps brun.

Charles Baudelaire

BAUDELAIRE

Come pretty kitty, come Baudelaire,
My poetic cat, Mr. Sex Appeal,
Curl on my lap a while while I stare
In your eyes of agate, your eyes of steel.

Put up your claws and let me caress
Your elastic back, your electric fur;
Oh, my hand is drunk with happiness,
Oh, which of us has begun to purr?

It's as if I looked into the eyes of my wife,
For her look is like yours, *cher* Baudelaire,
It's deep, it's icy, it cuts like a knife,

And from toe to head she seems to wear
A coffee aura, a dangerous musk
Cloaking her body like the dusk.

after Baudelaire, «Le Chat»

The Almost Ballade of the *Rennes d'Aujourd'hui*

Nous avons vu l'ombre du Mont Saint-Michel
Bénissant les eaux de la haute marée;
Nous avons vu les grands vitraux de Chartres
Saignant en rouge et bleu sous le soleil;
We've played at boules and baseball on the beach,
And shivered in the autumn rains of Rennes;
We've made new friends and talked to them of old,
And started planning how to come again.

We've lost and found ourselves on twisting streets,
And bought patisseries and Muscadet;
We've watched the changes of a foreign sky,
And thought of friendly places far away;
Nous sommes allés tels des soldats à l'école,
Ou tout le monde regarde les étrangers;
Nous avons espéré et essayé,
Et quelquefois, tout seuls, nous avons pleuré.

Nous nous sommes promenés à la campagne,
Cherchant des mûres, des pommes et des châtaignes;
Et quand nous sommes rentrés, main dans la main,
Nous savions que le voyage en vaut la peine;
We've gone to market, counting our francs and French,
And searched for a plumber on a Saturday;
We've read, made maps, written long letters home,
And felt the weight of all we couldn't say.

We've felt the weight of all we couldn't say,
Et quelquefois, tout seuls, nous avons pleuré;
Nous savions que le voyage en vaut la peine,
And started planning how to come again.

From *Still Here* (2008)

INTO PLACE

It's not so much a departure as an arrival,
Or rather, a having arrived—as when, out driving,
You pass an orchard on a southward hill,
Old apple trees aslant in heaps of prunings.
For Sale. What do you know of apples? Still,
One morning you wake up under a different ceiling

And feeling that you've not chosen but been chosen,
Are something less than owner, more than guest.
You fertilize and mow, attend the slow
Growth of apples readying for harvest,
And settle into place like leaves or snow,
Unfold like a letter delivered as addressed.

HOMING

Our fall has been a scourge of porcupines.
A neighbor says they're holed up in the shack
That rots in the woods behind the graveyard where
The Thynges are buried. At first, we found just signs:
Gnawed apples, broken branches. Then we woke
To a midnight rumbling in the barn and startled,
Head in a bag of Cortlands, one fat as a bear.
Gunless, we lured him into the Hav-a-Hart
With apple and peanut butter and lugged him away.
His family cruised the orchard in broad day.

≈

Abruptly the barking stopped; soon, head down,
The dog came shambling from the border brush
And up across the orchard. Our first glance showed
Her muzzled with what might have been a crown
Of thorns she'd nosed us from a neighbor's trash—
Like the hats, the gloves, the shirts that she brings home,
Sneakers, once a sheet; so the whole road
Knows, when something's missing, where to come.
She made no sound, but with a yellow paw
Waved vaguely now and then across her jaw.

≈

The vet raised pointed pliers. "You can thank
Her stars it isn't worse. Take a hound—
A hound keeps homing in when it's been quilled,
Gets stuck right down its throat." He braced, and yanked
A barb from the lolling tongue. Our eyes found
Each other's, then the poster of a horse,

Its parts all named in French. He laughed. "The skill
Is to be brutal"—yank; then yank. "Of course
Some dogs will learn, but others never will;
Instinct bites deep and holds, like hound or quill.

≈

Tonight the orchard is silent, empty; no
Strange scent enters to rouse us from the hearth
Where we and the dog are drowsing: subdued—or dreaming
That miles away in the swamp where we let them go
(Five in the end we trapped in the Hav-a-Hart)
The porcupines have gathered, are setting out
Through woods and fields and backyards, homing, homing,
Over river, past mall, across the Interstate,
To the rotting shed out where the dead Thynges lie
To set up house again, and multiply.

AFTER PRUNING

In this brown pause after the snow has melted,
Before the blunt thrust of bud and bulb,
We have this unhurried stooping along together
To gather the prunings.

Ahead, cut branches bristle around the trees;
Behind, the orchard stretches clean as a past
Without great sorrow, a future without surprises,
A well-swept floor.

Hour after hour we circle and circle the trees.
Our minds are nowhere, our minds are in our fingers
In the matted grass, the leaf-scraps and bits of bark,
Picking up sticks.

Some windless evening, they'll burn with a frantic crackle
And sting our bare arms with sparks as we feed the flames,
Then die to a scab of ash that will hoard for days
Its red-hot core.

But now in this pause after the snow has melted,
Before the blunt thrust of bud and bulb,
We have this unhurried stooping along together
So much like love.

CHILD IN THE HERB GARDEN

Exuberance of bird nor turn of worm
nor nuclear power plant beyond the curve
of eastward hill disturbs the child here curled
as if asleep among the herbs. Sky
crack, earth quake and siren bleat, still he'll
not wake to cry: sunlit, rainwashed,
buried in snow, observed or unobserved,
clenched kernel of this world, perfect stone.

THE POET AND THE WEATHERVANE

High on the ridgepole, Chanticleer
Spins as the fickle winds suggest
To survey his domain, north, south, east, west,
Crying (I fancy), "Here! Up here!
High on the ridgepole, Chanticleer!"

Down in the dusty pen, twelve mere
Mortal fowl peck unimpressed
By sickle tail and fat bronze breast.
They underlook the overseer
High on the ridgepole, Chanticleer.

Vain weathervane, cock without peer,
Let flightless fancies fill up the nest
With eggs for breakfast; you manifest
A poet's soul on your belvedere
High on the ridgepole, Chanticleer.

November: Sparing the Old Apples

Cracked urns of air, broken-winged umbrellas,
Black seabirds drying angular wings on a rock—
One with a hole through its trunk, another half-withered
As if it had suffered a paralytic stroke—
I should cut them down the orchard textbooks tell me
As a developer clearcuts tenements block by block,
And put in semidwarfs like his high-rent condominiums:
More apples the acre, easier to prune, spray, pick.

There they stand, fixed in impossible postures,
Like fugitives turned to stone for looking back
One last time at the place they must leave forever,
Or lords of an *ancien régime* condemned to the axe.

And I put my chainsaw away for another November
As if having endured conveyed some right to endure.

May 15

The time has come to revise
Line by line by line
The rough draft of my field
Till down the green grass lies
Obedient to design;
And the lovely scruffy tufts
Of flowers, they, too, must yield.

Prayer for December

Under this August sun
As plushly overblown
As some prize pumpkin in the gods' high garden,
Corn and tomatoes, row after row after row,

Lettuce, squash, beans
Blur in the sweat of our brows.
Clusters of grapes like udders droop from the vines
And the burden of apples bends down the apple boughs

Till the boughs break from the burden,
As we bend to breaking now.
Thin December, come, with your landscape hardened
By a reticent sun, come with the comfort of snow.

HOMESTEADER IN THE ORCHARD

What I've learned in these ten years, he thinks,
As he lays the teeth of the saw against the apple,
Is how to kill—without haste, without hesitation.
First the chickens, hung by the feet from a pinebranch,
Pinioned in plastic milkjugs with the bottoms cut out
So they couldn't flap as the blood drained into the bucket.

What I've learned in these ten years, he thinks,
As he draws the saw through its first irreversible stroke,
Is to kill without pleasure, to kill with gratitude.
The pigs next, fattened five months on grain and windfalls,
Then lured into cages, wrestled onto a pickup
And driven away, their squeals in the ears like knives

Through the opened beaks of chickens into the brain.
The sawteeth expose the orangey flesh of the tree,
A tree he knows well, as old as he or older,
But if he doesn't cut down the old trees, where can he set
The new for who may come after? What I've learned
In these ten years, he thinks, is how to die.

Now trees sprawl at all angles, McIntosh, Wagener,
Cortland, and he among them. In ten years, he thinks,
When they've long been cut up and split and have vanished as smoke
The smoke of blossoms will float on this slope each May.

"Still Here"

The visitor from Ireland said: the windless quiet.
Precisely the phrase I'd turned in my head all day.
Still here at dawn. The sun lips the orchard edge
And splashes new light through the open door of our bedroom.
The apple trees pose like dancers in a photograph.
Apples bead their branches like water that falls
And falls but the falls remain. The suspense of leaves!
Still here at noon. The dog sleeps under the car.
Still here at dusk. Closing the chicken coop
I look to the plum-dark sky as a great blue heron
Points the long ship of its body down toward the valley
And the silent river. Home. Still here when a friend
Calls to tell us a child at last has been born,
When a friend calls to tell us another friend has died.

Uncollected Poems

THE WORDS

—Let the words shape urns that will endure forever—

—Let them float out like blossoms from an apple—

—Slip into books like bodies into graves—

—Be thyme and garlic hanging from a rafter—

—When the covers open, let them leap out living—

—All winter sweeten like squash laid in the cellar—

—Shine like paintings in the mind's museum—

—Let them be eaten. Let them be forgotten—

APPROACH

The golfer settles his grip, adjusts his feet;
The iron hovers—flashes and wheels around,
And the ball's gone, the golfer's poised like a bow.
We lean to watch—then suddenly, "Look! There!"
A new world is hanging in the air,
While the green like an empty heaven waits below.
Still no one moves, till at last the ball comes down,
And the green rises, or seems to rise, and they meet.

In Parentheses

Midday. Midstream. Turning from my direction
I see upstream between two rows of trees
(Leaning over the river, seeming to hold it
Steady a moment in parentheses)

Iron arcing over the calm of water,
And from the water's calm, an arc of color
Answering, as if two pale red lips,
Parting to give a long-awaited answer,

Hesitated. Or as if they spoke
Unspeaking, by their moist and open waiting.
I lean against the rail a moment, steady,
Reading those pale red lips and hesitating.

NARCISSUS

Involved

in love

with the flex and firmness of my flesh

the smoothness of my skin

my dark caves and weedy places

I trace the curve of flank and thigh

inhale the odor

of forearms browned in the sun

inspect the small mole by my nose

delightful

why should I turn my attention

away from myself

or my image wherever I can find it

the bathroom mirror

the hungry eyes of a girl

your eyes as you listen

but I ask no one to share my pleasure

I am my own audience

my own critic

my reflections complete

a universe

Variation on a Theme by Baudelaire

It was a tanning salon deep underground
In a mazelike mall, at the end of a corridor
Where sullen young men lounged and chemical sound
Pulsed through the orange air. What was I there for?

I had no answers, but stretched on a sheet-draped cot
While a half-undressed attendant, mouthing sweet gum,
Laid her hand on my eyelids and I forgot
What I'd forgotten, knowing only the dumb

Pressure of light, the russet whisper of skin
And the breath of Doublemint mingled with My Sin.

THE TELEPHONE

You can have it in Verdant Green, in Nipple Pink,
In Robin's-egg Blue, in Flame, in Virgin White,
But a telephone's true color is black, black, black,
Ink-black, crow-black, coal-black like Arctic night.

It will sing to you in sweet electronic tones
Like a dentist's receptionist saying, "You may go *in* now,'
Or a dentist asking his receptionist out for a drink,
But a telephone's true voice is the rasp of a bow

Back and forth across nerves, who's there? who's there?,
Or the abrupt clangor that yanks you, poor flapping fish,
From your dreams, not knowing what you must answer for,
But knowing whatever it is, it's not what *you* wished.

Dazzled you stand there, holding the black, barbed hook,
And know that the knowledge thrilling the pith of your bones
You can never turn off like the TV, put down like a book.
When God calls his saints and his prophets, he telephones.

WHATEVER IT WAS

For her, spaces
Were for filling, questions
For answers, not mystery. When he'd given her a bowl
For its emptiness, she'd filled it
With flowers—as she'd filled so many evenings
With intense, inconsequential talk.
Now she'd gone off
Without a word, leaving him
Only a question, hanging
Like the one dress she'd left in the closet.
And now in the emptiness
Of early morning
As he skied the blue snow of the frozen river,
He thought of the first time he'd seen her
In the doughnut shop at 5:00 AM:
How she moved, moved, moved behind the counter,
Wiping it over and over
"To keep myself awake," she said.
(He'd been awake all night,
Watching late movies on television,
Sound turned off.)
And she laughed, and made him laugh, telling him
Of her crazy roommate who stayed home and played Bach all day
And her sane roommate who went out and played poker half the night,
And she made him tell her how he lived
Alone at the edge of the marsh
Where the deer came to graze in the moonlight and the wild turkeys
    had their paths.

After that he drove to the doughnut shop for breakfast every morning
Until the day she quit and came home with him.
She hung curtains in the windows, spread a rug over the linoleum,

Put flowers on the table, flowers on the bureau, flowers
In the big bowl he'd given her,
And that's the way it was, that's the way it was until
She was gone.
The sun was above the trees now.
One arm pushed a pole back, then the other,
One leg slid forward, then the other
Over the snow, and slowly
His mind emptied, he became
The clear sky, the frazzle of brush,
The slender tips of his skis,
The snow in all its unnamable colors.
Ahead the river stretched flat, on each side the marsh lay flat;
Shavings of snow ignited around him in the sunlight,
Then blinked out as he moved and the angle changed.
Oh, he could go on like this, he could go on
As long as the surface held, and the surface would hold
As long as winter lasted. And she—
Wherever she was—would find
Someone
Who would give her whatever it was she wanted,
Whatever it was she'd asked of him
And he didn't have.

PRAYER FOR THE SMALL ENGINE REPAIRMAN

Our Sundays are given voice
By the small engine repairman,
Whose fingers, stubby and black,
Know our mowers and tractors,
Chainsaws, rototillers,
Each plug, gasket and valve
And all the vital fluids.
Thanks to him our lawns
Are even, our gardens vibrant,
Our maples pruned for swings,
The underbrush whacked away.
"What's broke can always be fixed
If I can find the parts,"
He says as he loosens a nut,
Exposes the carburetor,
Tinkers and tunes until
To the slightest pull on the cord
The engine at once concurs.
Let him come into our homes,
Let him discipline our children,
Console and counsel our mates,
Adjust the gap of our passions,
The mix of our humors: lay hands
On the small engine of our days.

Afterwards, in the Parish Hall

Kip laughed and blinked red eyes and laughed again
At the story Richard told about his father,
While Leslie described her recent operation
To Jane, who'd asked, but didn't seem to listen.
Whose were those children dancing by the windows?
Constance, smiling gently, passed the brownies
To Adam, standing a bit apart and thinking
How always at funerals the person dead
Is the one who seems most present and substantial.

Kip blinked red eyes and laughed and blinked again
Telling Jason the story he'd heard from Richard.
Leslie asked Adam where he was at college.
Martha and Richard talked banks and advertising.
Whose were those children dancing by the windows?
Jane held Constance by a freckled wrist
To say how right the minister's words had been.
Then everyone shook hands a final time,
Told each other how too bad it was
It took a death to bring them all together,

Put on their overcoats and disappeared
From the bland and sunny space of their communion—
All but Charlie, vacuuming brownie crumbs
And wondering who they all were and where they'd come from.

The Verandah

From a neighbor's house, my daughter's laughter carries
Over the darkening water, and the deeper
Tones of the boy I tell her she'll someday marry,
Though she tells me she's known him forever,
No chance of romance, while solitary
On the verandah I watch the Necco-wafer-
Pink sun sink (oh, sentimental hour)
And from boat to boat the wrinkled water hurry
Whispering *Temporary, temporary*.

≈

Full moon high tide, the harbor brimful, quivering.
The evening quickens with the passionate cries
Of children, *Come on, come on,* and *Coming, coming,*
To kick the can or catching fireflies
Or lighting firecrackers on a string
To throw them from a float and get a rise
From pogies and dark watchers-from-verandahs,
Who bark a few clichés about the young
And then subside, ashamed, remembering.

≈

My mother had a sort of swinging divan
On which she glided through decades of summers
On the verandah, out of the mad-dog sun.
From it one day she watched her youngest plummet
Down from the sky like an angel heaved from heaven
Or sun-singed Icarus plunging from his summit.
Silent I fell—into a fortunate privet.
Silent she glided. The roof I knew forbidden,
And I knew myself neither condemned nor forgiven.

≈

No running on the pier or horseplay on the float;
An hour after meals before you swim;
Bait your own hook; no standing up in rowboats;
Never half-hitch the main sheet on the wind;
Voices carry over water, so don't shout.
Such were the laws, sensible and simple,
And from verandahs on the harbor's rim
Binoculars kept every child in sight
And registered what we did wrong or right.

≈

All day on the verandah my mother swayed
Like a sailboat from its mooring swaying,
Watching the sunlit stage on which we played
(Darkness lurking always in the wings,
For shimmering surfaces and friends betray)
And finding cause for praise in everything
But outboards, barking dogs, and children whining.
So with the easy tether of her gaze
She moored us in the casual drift of days.

≈

Sunset verandahs? Cocktails and philandering?
Not on this one, since I can remember.
Pandering, yes; verandah-sitters scanned
The stars and brought my wife and me together
One Sunday afternoon on the verandah.
A nice girl, a nice boy, and nearly neighbors,
You might have thought that we'd been friends forever
As we drank iced tea and shared a tuna sandwich
And began to ponder what our fates had planned.

≈

Night and day on the verandah, Love,
We hear the foghorn sounding from the Bay:
A mourning dove, you say, a warning dove,
Dark undertone to our complacent days.
What does it mourn, what does it warn us of,
Alone there in the middle of the waves,
Unmoving center of their mirrored maze,
Until our thoughts and dreams seem woven of
That sound as lonely as the loss of love.

≈

A summer house: a house of many rooms
Where the dead, the living and the still unborn
Mingle like jigsaw-puzzle pieces from
The box marked *Some are missing* that entertained
Our family through the annual three-day storm.
They brush against each other at each turning,
Presences familiar and unknown,
And on the verandah now a shadowy form
Seining for ghosts with his loose nets of rhyme.

OH, SAY CAN YOU SEE

This morning we walked the beach, the dog and I,
A morning so still that everything on the horizon
Floated on air like the new high-speed trains: islands, boats,
The lighthouse's admonishing finger in the bay.
And isn't it so, I wondered, that nothing truly touches,
Not ship and water, not lover and lover, not neutron and proton,
As the dog bounded after the skitter of plovers in air
Or swam towards mergansers serenely steaming away,
Her pleasure all in the chase, since never, never,
Could she dream to catch one.
                                            As we walked the long curve
Of the beach, over the rubble of stones, I thought again,
As so often, of a beach in Ireland where years ago
I wandered away from my wife and our children
(They were sitting legs out in the sand, and we'd formed the bodies
Of racing cars over them: *Vroom! Vroom!* they cried as I vanished)
To clamber a rocky headland in search of the curlews
Yeats had reproved in a poem—and find them,
The long downward curve of their beaks, their broken calls
Fading across the waves as they flew from me, symbols in Yeats
Of unfulfilled, unappeasable longing.
                                            And I came back again in memory
To the racing cars gone, wife and children gone,
Myself gone with them—carried off as in some Irish myth
To Tìr na nÓg, the country of the young.

What are we all but fictions?

Tonight the whole neighborhood gathered for the first night game
In the history of Thomas T. Tree stadium, brothers and sisters,
Parents, grandparents; hands over hearts we sang

"The Star-spangled Banner," faltering only in places,
Then played nine innings of laughter and arguments
With an umpire whose allegiance was transparently not to truth
But to beautiful symmetry, a tie game right to the end.
Floodlights glittered in the eyes of children up past their bedtimes
As we drove a whiffleball into the stars or the Tree,
Or missed it with a mighty blow, seeing the pitch only
In retrospect, when the catcher was holding the ball.
From across the harbor, Roman candles left over from the Fourth of July
Spattered the dark like applause.

THE PLEASURE OF SUMMER LIGHT

Over the white insouciance of yachts
like confetti on the water and the wide bright arcs
of waterskiers, over the mudflat clammers,
beachliers, porchsitters, grasscutters, over the bark -
ing dogs, the radio racket, the pock pop smack
of balls big and small, over the kites and the cookouts,
the gardeners bent to their lettuce, the snoozers in hammocks,
over the baby-blue tug with its coalbarge out by
the lighthouse, the children splashing in shallows, the joggers
and bicycle riders, over the rotary traffic
of minnows under the caucusing terns, and over
the cormorant stretching, stretching its long black neck
and lugging itself from the water over the white
insouciance of yachts, flies the old biplane,
Experience the Pleasure of Summer Light
trailing behind like a comic strip speech balloon.

IN DRUMCLIFFE CHURCHYARD

Under Ben Bulben's distant brow
Two children pose by Yeats's grave
Grinning, careless of the shadow
Curling over them like a wave
That rushes towards their sunstruck shallow
While underfoot the undertow

Tugs at bones long laid below.
Though our crazy hearts may rave
And insist it isn't so,
We know there's nothing we can save,
Mountains fall and children grow.
Snap the picture, then, and go.

GHOST STORY

All his alabaster lilypots. Mortar and pestle.
Aq. Dist. Fol. Laur. Te Virid.
—JAMES JOYCE, *ULYSSES*

1

1969; just arrived in Dublin,
Lost, two small children at our heels,
We wandered under the iron shadows of a railroad bridge
Past sootstained columns of a gaping church.
Seeing a chemist's, we went in—for what, I've forgotten—
To a dim and dusty room where high on shelves
Pale urns stood like gravestones with cryptic inscriptions
And a ghost in white coat regarded us over the counter
And said he didn't have whatever we wanted.
Outside, we soon found ourselves. Grafton Street was a new world.
We began to wonder if the shop had ever existed.
Later, reading *Ulysses*, a good tourist,
I realized we'd been in the chemist's where Leopold Bloom
Bought lemon soap in a fictional 1904.
"Chemists rarely move," he thought—
But when I looked for the place again, I couldn't find it.

2

Until 1992. Back in Dublin with my son,
I saw on the *Ulysses Map of Dublin* Sweny the Chemist's,
#6, on Lincoln Place. Yes, it was still there, though the urns were gone
And most of the dust.
A pleasant woman, no ghost, sold us lemon soap.

TOURIST IN THE COUNTRY

From somewhere in the leaves
Whose light and darker greens
Shifted like sunlit waves
A bird released its song

Across the afternoon.
Motionless, I stood
Until at last I'd found
The source of all that sound

Perched where twigs grew thick.
He sang and sang as if
My world did not exist
And the hedge were all of his,

While I cupped in my mind
Like water in the hands
The overflow of sound
And drank—the way I'd drink

In the village pub that night,
Silent and apart,
The strange, familiar talk
Of the locals at their darts.

BAND CONCERT IN REGENT'S PARK

I know the Titanic sank while the band played on,
But drifting in deck chairs over this swell of lawn
While the Royal Mechanical Engineers perform
Under a sort of Chinese Easter hat
Music as frivolous as the full-dress uniforms
In which by strength of will they do not sweat
Despite the insistent pressure of the sun,
Who can believe in sinking—or in the storm
That gathers, of course, in the west: rain before night;
And if music won't keep the ship from going down
Why should we try to keep the ship afloat
Except for the pleasure of hearing the final note?

To Canterbury

by the Pilgrims' Way

Foot-weary, pack-sore, we paused
As the long day faltered, where
At avenue's end a cathedral
Frosted the air

Like Bunyan's Celestial City.
It was for this we had come,
But now we turned from our vision
To look for a room

Where we could let fall the packs
We had lugged by highway, by lane,
Over stile and under low bough,
Uphill and down,

And the mud-crusted boots
That had lugged us in sunlight, in rain,
Through woodland, ploughland and pub,
And our crumpled jeans.

In tubs as big as coffins
We lay a half-hour like the dead,
Washed off the mud and the soreness,
And rose renewed.

Tomorrow would bring the cathedral
Where Becket was killed, where the king,
Barefoot, in burlap, prayed;
Choirboys would sing.

But tonight we'd eat well and lie easy
In praise of the ancient route
And of boots and bluejeans and bodies
Worn thin but not out.

THE HOUSE BY THE RAILROAD TRACKS

How the trains go boring down the tracks, hell-bent
To get wherever the rails are taking them;
At night they're a roaring of blood in our ears, at dawn
When the sunlight triggers the birds into song again,
They pass with a roaring of blood, wheels against rails,
Going round, going on, going round, going on, going round.
They'll be back at the same times tomorrow, with us and the birds.

Think of how green surprised us again this spring,
Of the birds' insistent *Listen to this, to this,*
Of the girls and boys we saw today in the park
At their first, bird-like flirting. Say to them, That research
Has been done and published a thousand times before?
Do you hear it again, the roaring of blood in our ears?
The ten o'clock train is boring down through the dark.

MARITAL SEX

1

Watching the Eclipse from the Bedroom Window

Three spheres slide precisely into place.
Shadow of earth brings blood to the pale moon's face.
Celestial rhyming! What metaphor for this
Collusion of heavenly bodies but heavenly kiss?

A distant kiss. And perverse—three pairs of lips.

Five, counting ours. Love, let's eclipse the eclipse.

2

Gestures of Love

Now that we've made love, you turn your back
And settle into sleep. I lie alone.
My fingers trace you, curving like a hook
Hung in deep waters, all its soft bait gone.

3

Aubade after Twenty-five Years

Somewhere halfway down the closet, my pants turn to your pants.
Mine on top, yours on top, our sweaters have sex on the shelves.
My foot pokes a hole in your sock, you're lost in my shirt
As laughing in half-light we try to unscramble ourselves.

SKIERS

We break an old trail through new snow
Under high, snow-heavy trees
Cautious on the hush of skis.
This, I think, is how we go,
Still and still, slow and slow,

Pushing down a trail we know,
New again in fallen snow,
You ahead and I behind,
I ahead and you behind.
This, I think, is how we go.

This, I think, is how we go,
I ahead and you behind,
You ahead and I behind,
New again in fallen snow,
Pushing down a trail we know,

Still and still, slow and slow.
This, I think, is how we go—
Cautious on the hush of skis
Under high, snow-heavy trees
We break an old trail through new snow.

VALEDICTION

Now the bumbling bees that hover
Over loveliness in flower
Important with their store of pollen
Have had their hour;

Time has come for you to shed your
Silken petals and declare
Whether you are apple, cherry,
Plum or pear,

And all summer take your pleasure
Nourishing the ripening fruit
With the sun and rain you welcome
Through leaf, through root.

REFUTING BERKELEY

Then when I stared through glass at the figment of flesh that
Could have been anyone's baby but was mine, the doctor
Told me—a pebble only—I stood mutely:
I had no idea.

Later I watched you feeding at your mother's
Small breasts swollen with the milk you'd brought her,
A weight like stone in the hollow under my breastbone,
But no idea.

Reality, said Berkeley, is *all* idea: matter
Exists in perception only. But Samuel Johnson,
Kicking a stone "with mighty force," declared
"I refute it *thus.*"

And now when the door whaps suddenly open and you are
Home with a couple of friends like wind made visible
For a coat, to pat the dog, tell us some story, and
Are suddenly gone,

As the little car drives off overflowing with
Elbows and laughter, I stand in the doorway staring
Into the dark and the invisible wind
And have no idea.

GRADUATION SPEECH

Like much that matters, baking bread is easy
Enough, with good ingredients, a simple recipe:
To water, sweetener, salt and yeast
Add flour, and mix. Oh, yes, there's Mystery,
But who demands to understand
When the dough is answering the hand
Under a morning window facing east?
Do they teach this at the University?

Cover the dough—left in the dark alone
It knows to take the next step on its own.
And when it's risen with the sun
Towards noon an hour or two, punch it back down,
Shape it into loaves, and wait
Again while it again grows great—
But not too great: just peers above the pan.
Then, as the good book says, "Bake until done."

The Zen of loafing? Eat a metaphor?
Now's the time to try if bread is more
Than bread alone. Taste. Devour.
Firmly yielding? Moist and crunchy? Or
Evidence scattered on the plate
Of a loaf the knife disintegrates?
You've made it, anyhow. The day is yours—
Yours and the sun's, now at its tallest hour.

THE MERGER

for my son

Trying to think of something useful
To say about marriage, I remember
A morning when I was twenty-plus,
Self-absorbed in my tinny pink
Renault Dauphine, my Little Toot,
And I tried to get by a tank-truck on
A bendy road too briefly straight.
Shuddering, pedal floored, my frivolous
Vessel leveled with the cab
Like a pilot fish by a shark's grim grille.
Then there was a car ahead of us
And, as I tried to floor a pedal
Already on the floor, the blue
Of ice I hadn't seen. Spinning
Toward the implacable hugeness of the cab, looking up
Into the eyes of the truckdriver, I felt
Only the sweet certainty of
Submission, call it love, as if
Already I had left myself and could look
Down with the driver's godlike and loving
Eyes at a comical pink Dauphine
Sliding backwards down the road, then spinning
Again and into a snowbank, tilted
Against a tree. One flat tire
And a dent in the roof I pushed out myself.
I made it to work on time. Because
The truckdriver had seen the oncoming car
Before I had, had seen the patch of blue

And had slowed to let me by, I met
And married your mother, and you were born
And have grown up to meet and marry, and I
Have begun to understand the blind
Release of self to the will of another
And the answering wise, dispassionate
Restraint of the merger we call marriage.

Random Crumbs

for my grandson

Fourth Wolsey of an undistinguished line,
Two grandfathers, your father, and now you, Ben,
Two at least lovers of Yeats and of the prayer
He made for his daughter when seawinds shook his tower
With savagery that matched those savage times—
Savage like these, when might and madness clash
And men's high constructs wilt to heaps of ash.
Can I raise a lasting tower with weak-kneed rhymes?

You make us grateful, Ben, for the unplanned,
The happy haphazard, cannily uncanned,
Pick-up shinny on pond ice, off the cuff,
Evens made odd, ununiformed, let's say scruff-
Y. Forget the futile quest for better, best.
Did It that made the world, when It was done,
Lift a fierce fist and cry, "I'm Number One"?
Seeing the work was good, It took a rest.

That good, still good enough, is underfoot.
Grip deep, hold fast, a dandelion root.
May you and your lover someday make a house
With room for the daily serendipitous,
Birth to death, all life's holy mess.
Let your mouse be Stuart, or one who comes
From the wall at night to scavenge random crumbs
Like a poet's inspiration. To it, success.

A WHISPER, A CRY

This is the Census Taker's month. He comes
Bearing his great grey slate to do his sums.

Now no answer where the knocker drops
Or a dim whisper: "Finished. Here Time stops."

Now a newborn cries out, "Here. Come in.
Let me be numbered and let Time begin."

Children Walking a Rail

Leaving, we hugged him good-by,
His body gone all bone
As if we hugged the nubby

Trunk of maple, oak.
Three days, and he receded
Into the final coma

And we began to see
Through him, as when surprised
Through naked October trees

By a landscape barely recognized
We know has been there always.
Tonight when we visit his wife

We'll struggle to keep balance,
Remembering, letting go,
Three children walking a rail

Hands held wide, and open.

WHAT IS LEFT

Picture her ice-box, stuffed with half-empty
Jars—horseradish, olives, pickles—packets
Of long-outdated yeast:
A place to forage for a pick-up feast.
Nothing in life comes out exactly,

Something is left to carry. Picture the yarn
Filling her basket, odd ends of every color
She knit without a pattern,
Flowers and comets starting under
Her fingers like four-year-olds released

To choose their yarn from the basket
And shape it to a spiral on the sand.
Spiraling in, or out?
Picture her a child in a bomb-pocked land
Spiraling with a basket for flowers to carry

Home. Something is always left.

Wolsey's Hole

Somewhere on a stream in Vermont, a cold
Bright stream bellying black over boulders
And ruffling cowlicks of foam, a live slick
Stream, a lithe quick stream like a rope thrown down,
Is a hollow carved by an eddy into the sheer
Granite under a fall—a wetwalled pocket,
Stone sink that for sixty years my cousins have known
As Wolsey's hole—because my father, sixty summers ago,
Slipped into it swimming and couldn't get out, I was told
Last summer by a cousin's cousin. Oh, when I heard,
How there arose from some hole in my heart a magnificent bellow,
Cold and afraid and delighted! I heard the laughter
From faces rimming the hollow, I saw the knotted
Rope let down, and my father hauled out glowing
In his baggy trunks, freckled and shaking, red hair aflame
In sunlight. And I thought: Can I learn
To think of death not as infinite contraction,
Curtains closed over midnight, but as curtains drawn back
To let in the moon and the stars, the whole horizon,
To let in the dead and the living—a rope thrown down
To haul me from the hole of my heart, all dripping and shining?

THE SOBER BOAT

"Poor preparation makes for piss-poor performance." The friend
Who used to live by that is dead, his boat gone down
On a weekend cruise along the coast of Maine:
A collision in the fog, a violent squall,
Some sudden failure of the hull—
Nothing ever found but the three drowned men.

Poor preparation makes for piss-poor performance. But the one
Safe bet is, every identity ends.
No craft avoids that for long; the question's not when,
But how. Imagine a storm,
Sky darkening, waves in an uproar,
Lifting and closing in like tenements,
Like black fists, raw mouths,
Flames, smoke, dreams of forgotten guilt,
Hot eyes prizing, prizing at the skin
Till something gives. And then
The water starts its working on the men.
The question's not when, but how.

The grace of boats is the leanness of their curves,
Their subtle tightness and the way they ride
Part of the waves and apart; but in the end
They're lost somehow, no matter how well made.
Poor preparation makes for piss-poor performance. Style
Is a last word, is a signature of love.

WHITE DOGWOOD

All those boring passages of description
She used to skip in novels, when was it they
Began to be all she remembered,
All that remained when action, then character
(She'd loved the action, but her teachers
Praised character; character is fate, they intoned)
Slipped from her mind? A farmhouse, for instance,
On the Mediterranean, a few chickens
Scratching the dry grass of a courtyard, a cove
Tucked among rocks, and inland, from a pocket
Between hills, the sound of bells.
Two figures sitting a long time on a bench
By the open door. Who were they, what were they saying?
Then a scene by moonlight, a shadow slanting
Against a stucco wall . . . So, when she noticed
The stone gone from the ring—in the garden? the sink?—
She didn't grieve long. What mattered, it seemed,
Was the ring itself, the loosened grip
Implying diamond. And so she imagined
Slipping some night from their bed and disappearing
Into the roses and lettuce, and the white dogwood
Flowering there in the dark beside the cedar.

RESOLUTION

When the tsunami draws back its fistful of waters
And crushes the city, let me for once be ready.
Let me be washing the dishes or patting the dog.

When the great windstorm angles across the flatlands
Hungry and howling, let me be patting the dog.
Let me be kneading the bread or picking an apple.

When the ground shudders and splits and all walls fall,
Let me be writing a letter or kneading the bread.
Let me be holding my lover, watching the sunrise.

When the suicide bomber squeezes the trigger
And fierce the flames spurt and wild the body parts fly,
Let me be holding my lover or drinking my coffee.

Let us be drinking our coffee, unprepared.

ACKNOWLEDGMENTS

The poems in this collection, some in differing versions, have been
   previously published by the following journals:

The American Scholar: Random Crumbs

Atlanta Review: Homing; Prayer for the Small Engine Repairman;
   Resolution

The Atlantic Monthly: Relativity

The Beloit Poetry Journal: The Verandah; Wolsey's Hole

Blue Unicorn: Aubade after Twenty-five Years; In Drumcliffe Churchyard;
   Variation on a Theme from Baudelaire; What is Left

The Cape Rock: The Merger

The Christian Century: Afterwards, in the Parish Hall; A Whisper, a Cry

The Christian Science Monitor: After Pruning

Commonweal: Evening Meditation in a Cathedral Town; Fibonacci
   Sequence; Graduation Speech; November: Sparing the Old Apples;
   On the Beauty of the Universal Order

Compass Rose: Ghost Story; In Parentheses

Country Journal: Into Place

The Formalist: The Poet and the Weathervane

Harvard Magazine: Stones

Hellas: The House by the Railroad Tracks

The Hiram Poetry Review: Approach; Refuting Berkeley; Thirty-five

Light: Baudelaire; The Pleasure of Summer Light; Watching the Eclipse
   from the Bedroom Window

Light Year '86: L'Oiseau, La Souris, et le Chat; The Bird, the Mouse, and
   the Cat

The Literary Review: Band Concert in Regent's Park; The Bliss of Bears;
   Child in the Herb Garden; The Quiet of the Country; The Sober Boat;
   The Telephone; To Canterbury

The Lyric: Valediction

Mazagine: The Infestation

The Pennsylvania Review: Homesteader in the Orchard

Penumbra: Narcissus

Piedmont Literary Review: Prayer for December

Poet Lore: Children Walking a Rail
Poetry: May 15
Poetry International: Skiers
Poetry Northwest: Winter Squash
Puckerbrush Review: "Still Here"; Tourist in the Country;
    White Dogwood
Rivendell: Oh, Say Can You See
Shenandoah: Gestures of Love
Soundings East: For Sarah
Southern Poetry Review: Whatever It Was

The text of "Le Chat" is taken from Charles Baudelaire, *Les Fleurs du Mal*,
    Paris, Calmann-Levy, Editeurs, 1868.

AUTHOR'S THANKS

As always, I am grateful to family, friends and fellow-poets for support
and counsel. I owe particular thanks to Frank Reeve for his suggestions
about and enthusiasm for the manuscript I sent him, and to Sid Hall for
choosing this book to inaugurate his Granite State Poetry Series and for
producing it so handsomely.

ABOUT THE AUTHOR

Born in Concord, Massachusetts, CHARLES W. PRATT *attended Phillips Exeter Academy for his high school years, and then returned there to teach in the 1960s. In the early 1980s, he and his wife Joan bought an apple orchard in nearby Brentwood, which they have operated ever since. They are currently working to turn over the orchard to new owners, in order to keep it alive.*

The central poems of his first book, In the Orchard *(Tidal Press, 1986, with drawings by Arthur Balderacchi) were written with the encouragement of an Individual Artist Grant from the New Hampshire State Council on the Arts; his chapbook* Still Here *(winner of the Finishing Line Press Prize in Poetry) followed in 2008.*

In 1975–76, the Pratts spent a year in Rennes, France, while he taught at School Year Abroad, a program for American students of high-school age. Their resultant affection for the French language, landscape and people was responsible for Fables in Two Languages and Similar Diversions, *which was published in 1994.*

The Pratts have two children and five grandchildren.

THE HOBBLEBUSH GRANITE STATE
POETRY SERIES

*HOBBLEBUSH BOOKS publishes several New Hampshire
poets each year, poets whose work has already received
recognition but deserves to be more widely known. The
editors are Sidney Hall Jr. and Rodger Martin.
For more information, visit the Hobblebush
website: www.hobblebush.com.*